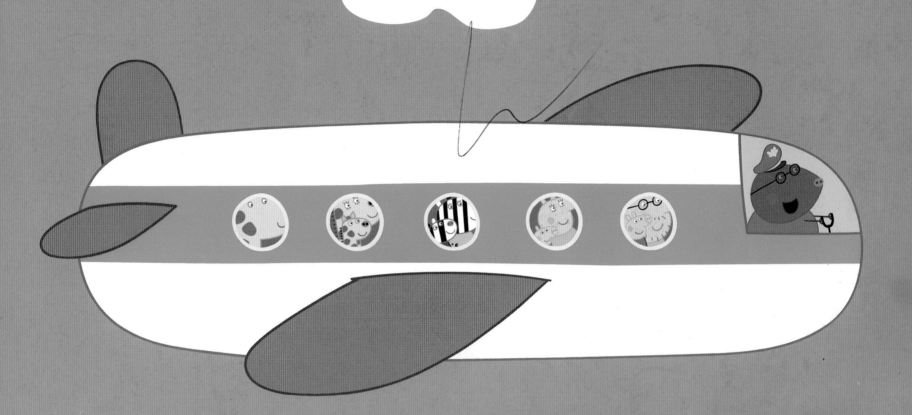

This holiday book belongs to

....

LADYBIRD BOOKS

UK | USA | Canada | Ireland | Australia | India | New Zealand | South Africa

Ladybird Books is part of the Penguin Random House group of companies
whose addresses can be found at global.penguinrandomhouse.com.

www.penguin.co.uk   www.puffin.co.uk   www.ladybird.co.uk

Penguin
Random House
UK

First published 2020
001

Printed in China

A CIP catalogue record for this book is available from the British Library

ISBN: 978-0-241-41225-1

All correspondence to:
Ladybird Books
Penguin Random House Children's
One Embassy Gardens, New Union Square
5 Nine Elms Lane, London SW8 5DA

Peppa's Summer Holiday

Peppa was at playgroup, and she was feeling very excited. "I'm going on a summer holiday!" she cried. "Me, too!" shouted all of Peppa's friends. "I'm going to swim in a swimming pool," cried Peppa.

"Me, too!" shouted all of Peppa's friends.
Everyone was going on a summer holiday, and
everyone was going to swim in a swimming pool.

After playgroup, Peppa and George packed their holiday bags. "Please could you help me pack my flamingo, Daddy?" asked Peppa. "Of course," said Daddy Pig, trying to squeeze Peppa's inflatable flamingo into her bag.

"Why don't we deflate it first?" suggested Mummy Pig.
"Great idea, Mummy Pig!" said Daddy Pig.

Peppa, George, Mummy Pig and Daddy Pig put their bags
in the car and headed to the airport.
"We're going on holiday! We're going on holiday!" sang Peppa,
over and over again.

"It seems like everyone's going on holiday!"
said Daddy Pig. "Just look at all this traffic!"

Peppa and her family made it to the airport just in time.

They quickly showed their passports to Miss Rabbit, and then put their bags through the scanning machine.

"Yippee!" cheered Peppa and George
when they boarded the aeroplane.
"Phew, we made it," said Mummy Pig,
as everyone put on their seatbelts.

When they arrived at the hotel, everyone was very excited.
"Look at the blue sea," gasped Daddy Pig.
"Look at the palm trees," sighed Mummy Pig.
"Look at the swimming pool!" cried Peppa.

"Let's find our room," said Mummy Pig.
"Then we can go swimming."
"Hooray!" cheered Peppa and George.

After they had unpacked their bags in their room,
Peppa, George and Daddy Pig jumped straight
into the swimming pool. Meanwhile, Mummy Pig
relaxed in the sunshine with an ice-cold smoothie.

Peppa and George found Emily and Edmond Elephant
splashing about in the water.
"What are **you** doing here, Emily?" said Peppa.

Splish!

Splash!

"I'm on holiday," said Emily. "What are YOU doing here?"
Peppa giggled. "I'm on holiday, too!"
"Dine-saw SPLASH!" cried George, splashing Edmond.
The swimming pool was lots of fun.

Soon Miss Rabbit arrived at the pool
and made an announcement.
"Attention please! This afternoon's holiday
activity is a visit to a turtle sanctuary."

"Oooh!" gasped the children.
"If turtle hatchlings are being released into the sea today, we may be able to watch from a distance!" said Miss Rabbit.

On the turtle trip, Peppa and Emily saw Rebecca and Richard Rabbit.
"What are YOU doing here, Rebecca?" said Peppa.
"I'm on holiday," replied Rebecca. "What are YOU doing here?"
"I'm on holiday, too!" said Peppa.

Peppa, Emily and Rebecca loved watching the baby turtles going for their first swim in the sea.
"Can we go to the pool with Rebecca now, Mummy?" asked Peppa.
"Of course," said Mummy Pig.

The next day, Peppa and George went straight to the pool.
"Suzy! Zoe!" cried Peppa. "What are YOU doing here?"
"We're on holiday!" replied Suzy Sheep and Zoe Zebra.

Miss Rabbit announced that the next activity would be a jungle walk to find sloths. "Oooh!" gasped the children.

Splish!

Splash!

Peppa was very good at spotting sloths, and she also spotted the Giraffe family!

It was very hot in the jungle.
"Please can we go back to the swimming pool now, Mummy?" said Peppa.
"Of course," replied Mummy Pig. "It'll be nice to cool off in the pool."

After the jungle trip, everyone jumped into the pool.

"Our last holiday activity is a dance competition," said Miss Rabbit, "in the swimming pool!"

Hee!

Hee!

Peppa was very excited and started to dance.
"Look at me – I'm doing a flamingo dance!" she cried.
The children laughed and copied Peppa's funny
flamingo dance.

Soon everyone was doing Peppa's funny flamingo dance . . . even the grown-ups! Miss Rabbit picked up her megaphone. "And the winning dance is . . . Peppa's flamingo dance!"

"HOORAY!"
everyone cheered.

Everyone had enjoyed
their holiday, but it was
time to go home.

Once everyone was on the aeroplane, Miss Rabbit announced, "I'm afraid take-off has been delayed."
"Can we go to the swimming pool?" asked Peppa.
Mummy Pig frowned. "I'm afraid not, Peppa."

"You **could** do the flamingo dance though,"
suggested Daddy Pig.
"Yes!" cried Peppa, and she started to dance . . .

Soon, everyone on the aeroplane was doing Peppa's flamingo dance . . . right up until it was time for take-off.

Everyone loved their summer holiday, and everyone loved Peppa's flamingo dance!